The Chimpanzees of Happytown

For Victoria,
who makes our lives a Happytown
G.A.

To my lovely wife, Sarah,
with love
G.P-R.

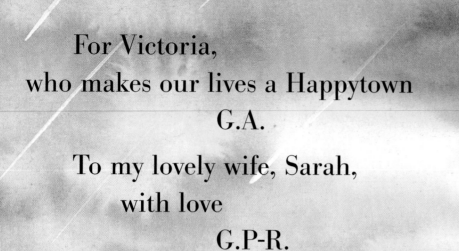

ORCHARD BOOKS
338 Euston Road, London NW1 3BH
Orchard Books Australia
Hachette Children's Books
Level 17/207 Kent Street, Sydney, NSW 2000

ISBN 978 1 84616 467 5

First published in 2006 by Orchard Books
First published in paperback in 2007

A CIP catalogue record for this book is available from the British Library.

10 9 8 7 6 5 4 3 2 1

Printed in China

Orchard Books is a division of Hachette Children's Books

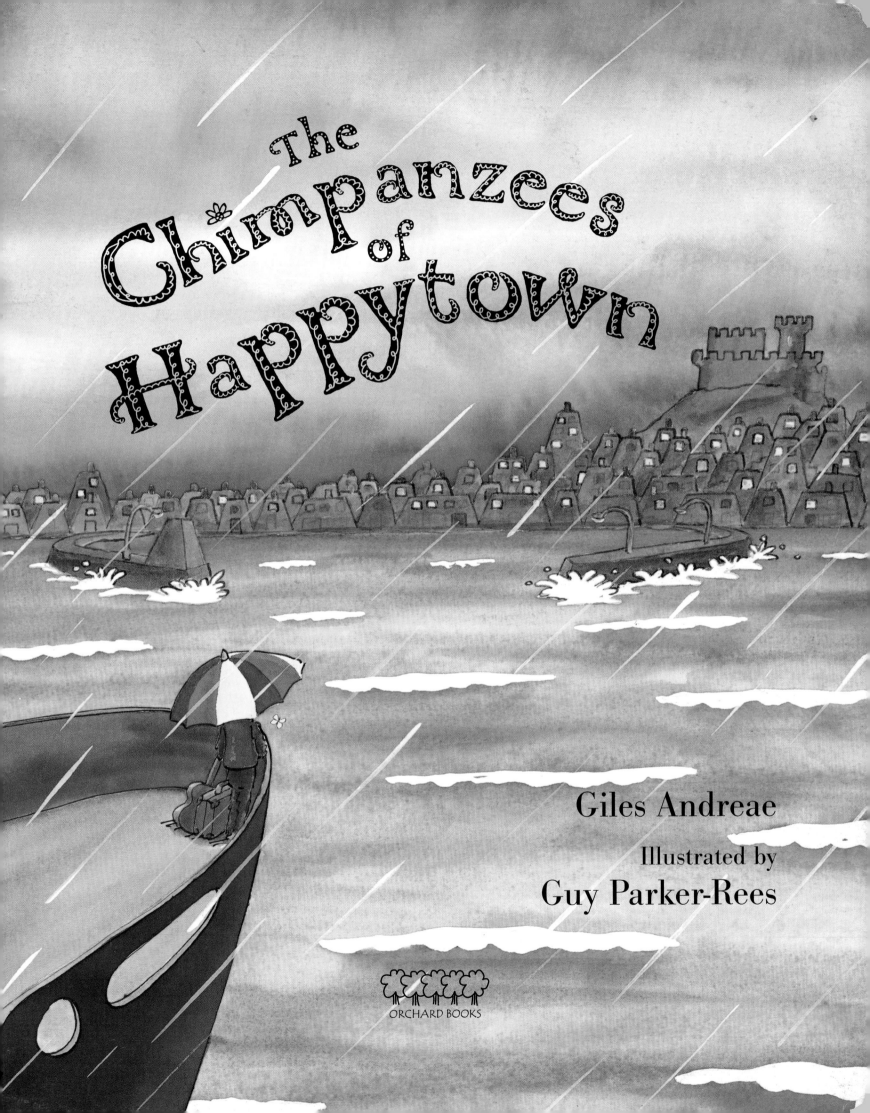

The Chimpanzees of Happytown

Giles Andreae

Illustrated by
Guy Parker-Rees

ORCHARD BOOKS

There was a town not far from here
Called Drabsville, USA,
Where all the houses looked the same
And all of them were grey.

There were no parks to play in.

There were no trees at all.

And the chimpanzees who lived there
All felt very sad and small.

Now, Chutney was a traveller.

He travelled far and wide.

And he came home with a box one day,

Which had a seed inside.

He planted it

and watered it

And watched it slowly grow –

Until, one day, the mayor looked down
And shouted, "No,
NO,
NO!"

From way up in his palace
He had spotted Chutney's seed.
And now he bellowed, "Chop it down!
Destroy that ghastly weed!"

"You can't grow things in Drabsville.
That is just beyond the pale!
Guards, seize that wretched chimpanzee
And throw him into jail!"

So Chutney went to prison,
Where his cell was cold and bare.
And the mayor left for his winter break
To catch some country air.

But meanwhile, back at Chutney's house,
The boy and girl next door

Said, "We must water Chutney's seed

And make it grow once more."

And, with the children's love and care,

It wasn't very long

Before the seed stretched out its shoots

And grew up tall and strong.

And Chutney, from his prison cell,
Looked out one day to see
The leaves and flowers and branches
Of his own beloved tree.

It gave him strength.

It gave him hope.

It made him happy too.

And when, at last, they let him out
He said, "There's work to do!"

"Chimpanzees, this town is dead.
These streets are all the same.
Let's celebrate our differences.
Let's make it fun again!

Let's make our houses colourful.
Let's pull our fences down.
And, while we're at it, why not change
Its name to
Happytown?"

The chimpanzees fell silent.

These were stirring words to hear.

"He's right," they said. "That Chutney's right!"

And they began to cheer.

"I'm going to paint mine pink," one said.
"That's what I'm going to do.

Then I'm going to climb up on the roof
And paint the chimney blue!"

"My windows will look fabulous
Without those iron bars,
And the walls will be a symphony
Of flowers and hearts and stars!"

Then Chutney stopped and looked up
At the palace of the mayor.
"The children need a place to play,"
He said. "Let's build it there."

So they pulled the palace down
And built a playground with some swings,

A roundabout,

a rocket ship

And loads of other things.

"Let's have a party," Chutney said,
"With yummy things to eat!"
There were sausages and ice cream.
There was dancing in the street.

And everyone was happy now
Except, of course, the mayor,
Who came back to his palace.
But his palace wasn't there.

"What's happened here?" he said. "Enough!
Guards, seize them, every one!"
But the guards, of course, just laughed
And said, "We're having too much fun!"

So they put the mayor in prison,
Where he settled in quite well –

Until, one day,
the new mayor came
And opened up his cell.

Mayor Chutney said, "You see my tree?
Well, now I hope you know
That everything that we cut down
Will find a way to grow."

"And things will always blossom
If we dare to set them free.

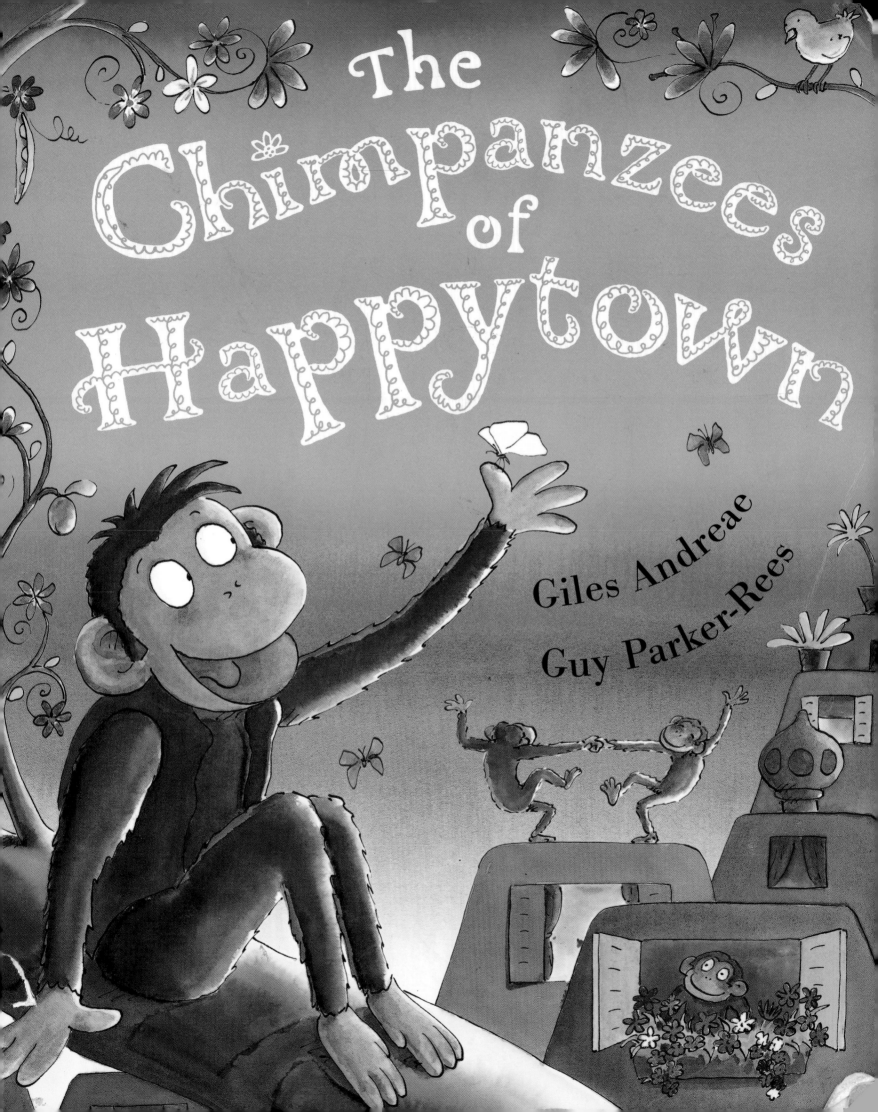

It's no different for a little flower
As for a chimpanzee."